Frustrating Day

Published by Advance Publishers, L.C.
www.advance-publishers.com

Written by K. Emily Hutta
Art layout by J.J. Smith-Moore
Art composition by David Maxey
Produced by Bumpy Slide Books

ISBN: 1-57973-084-1

Blue's Clues Discovery Series

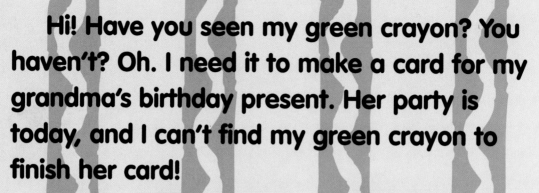

Hi! Have you seen my green crayon? You haven't? Oh. I need it to make a card for my grandma's birthday present. Her party is today, and I can't find my green crayon to finish her card!

I feel . . . kind of mad . . . and sad.

Frustrated! That's it!
Do you ever feel frustrated?
Yeah. It doesn't feel
very good.

Well, you know what to do when things get frustrating, right? Yeah! Stop, breathe, and think. Okay. I'm stopping. I'm taking a deep breath. And I'm thinking about where my green crayon could be.

Oh! That's right! I always put my green crayon in Sidetable Drawer when I put my notebook away. Here it is! And now I don't feel frustrated.

Blue, do you ever feel frustrated? What frustrates you? Oh, okay! We'll play Blue's Clues to figure out what makes Blue feel frustrated. Will you help me? You will? Great!

What's that? You see a clue? Where?
Yeah! On the bow. What do you think a bow
has to do with what makes Blue feel frustrated?
Hmmm. Let's see if we can find two more clues.

Hey! We know what to do when you're frustrated. Do you remember? Yeah! Stop, breathe, and think.

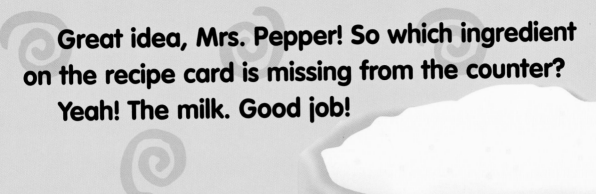

While Mr. Salt and Mrs. Pepper are finishing their cake, I'll just finish this card for my grandma. There! What do you think?

Yeah, I like it, too. Oh, you see a clue! Where? A lace. So what do you think a bow and a lace have to do with what frustrates Blue? Yeah, I think we need to find our last clue.

Hey! Have you seen Blue?

Here you are, Blue! Hi, Slippery. What's the matter?

Whoa! Hi, Steve. I can't get my boat to sail. I've been blowing and blowing, but it just won't go. I'm about to give up.

Wow! Another frustrated friend. What do you think Slippery should do? Yeah! Stop, breathe, and think.

What do you think Slippery can use to get his boat to move? Good thinking! He can use the oars! You are so smart!

Well, we've helped out all of our frustrated friends—except for Blue. We still need to find one more clue.

No, we're not looking for a shoe—we're looking for a clue. Oh! The clue is my shoe! We have all three clues! You know what that means? It's time to go to our . . . Thinking Chair!

Okay. We're trying to figure out what makes Blue frustrated. Our clues are a bow, a lace, and a shoe. So what could make Blue feel frustrated? That's it! Blue feels frustrated about learning to tie her shoes! We just figured out Blue's Clues!

And now I think we can help Blue. I had trouble learning to tie my shoes, too. But then my friends taught me this rhyme:

Make one of Blue's ears,
And another of Blue's ears.
Then do-si-do.
Now we have a Blue's Clues bow!

With a little practice, I think Blue can do it, don't you?

Hey! Blue's not frustrated anymore. In fact, nobody is. We all feel great, and just in time for Grandma's birthday party, too.

Thanks for helping us figure out Blue's Clues!

BLUE'S "TIE YOUR OWN SHOE"

You will need: a shoe, a shoelace, a hole punch, a piece of cardboard bigger than the shoe, scissors, and paint, crayons, or markers

1. Put a shoe on the cardboard and trace the shape with a pencil.

2. Ask a grown-up to cut out the shoe shape you just drew and punch six holes in the cardboard shoe, two by two.

3. Decorate your "shoe" any way you want to.

4. Lace the shoelace through the holes (you might need a little help with this, too).

5. Practice tying the laces of your cool new "shoe" by using the rhyme Steve taught you:

Make one of Blue's ears,
And another of Blue's ears.
Then do-si-do.
Now we have a Blue's Clues bow!